By The Queen

As told to Daphne Skinner

Illustrated by John Kurtz

1

It's Not Easy Being a Stepmom

Let's get a few things straight. I adored Snow White. I still do. Whatever you've heard—that I was an "evil stepmother" who tried to harm her—is completely false. Everything I did, I did for her own good. And when I tell my side of the story, I know you'll believe me.

First of all, unless you've raised a teenage girl yourself, you have no idea what an ordeal it can be. Teenage girls are lazy. They're impolite. They eat junk. They dress like gypsies. And they need constant supervision, because they're boy crazy. Snow White was a typical teen. Maybe you've heard differently. But if there's one thing I'm known for, it's being a straight shooter.

Second, I was her *step*mother. Stepmothers have a bad reputation. They're often called "cruel," or "wicked." For some reason, the world hates them. Why? I don't know.

But I do know this: a "real" mother can get testy every now and then, and nobody raises an eyebrow. But if a stepmother loses her temper just once, it's on the front page of *The Medieval Times*.

Finally, I'm a widow. I'm not asking for your sympathy, believe me. But when my husband died, I was left to raise Snow White—all by myself. I was a hardworking single parent who didn't get a speck of help from anybody. And when things went wrong, I got all the blame. Read on and see for yourself.

The Medieval Times
HANSEL AND GRETEL MEANT THE WORLD TO ME!

2

Healthful Exercise

People have said I was vain, but of course I wasn't. Not in the least. I just happen to have the gift of true beauty, and that silly Magic Mirror likes to tell me about it all day long. "You're the fairest one of all." Blah, blah, blah. As if I didn't know it! (I'm just being honest.)

I guess because I take a healthy interest in my appearance, I expected Snow White to do the same. How wrong I was! She wore the same ragged-looking dress day after day. She ate the most unhealthy food. And she never, ever exercised.

I knew I had to take matters in hand. My darling little stepdaughter needed discipline. She needed a regimen. She needed exercise. In short, she needed my help. And I was going to give it to her, whether she liked it or not.

I spoke to her right away.

"You're a growing girl," I said. "You need your exercise. Start by hauling one hundred buckets of water down to the dungeon." (I renovated after the funeral, and now it's my office.)

To my amazement, Snow White wasn't the least bit grateful. Here I was, giving her the opportunity to get some muscle tone and burn off all kinds of calories, and she whined. She said the work was "hard." After thirty trips up and down the stairs, she even pretended to faint!

I am nothing if not reasonable, so I let her rest for a few moments. Then I gave her the easiest job in the palace, washing the front steps. It's great aerobic exercise (I'd love to do it myself if only I had the time), and I thought she'd be pleased.

Wrong again.

I stepped away for a moment to consult my mirror, and when I returned, Snow White had stopped working. She was lounging on the steps, staring into space, and humming! Then—and this really rattled me—she started talking to the birds!

No wonder I worried about her.

3

A Wholesome Diet

Things got worse. The next day, when she was supposed to be scrubbing the kitchen floor, I found Snow White gobbling down a piece of cake.

"Give that to me," I demanded, snatching it away. "Cake is unsuitable for growing girls. It's full of fat and sugar, and it will rot your teeth down to nubbins."

Then I reminded her how lucky she was to be on her new diet of bread and gruel. It couldn't be healthier—it's low in calories, sugar- and fat-free, and chock-full of trace minerals. Our livestock thrives on it. I'd be on it myself if it weren't for my allergies.

"Another month or two," I promised, "and you'll be as strong as a bull! You'll be taking the stairs like a mountain goat, three at a time! With full buckets! Won't that be wonderful?"

She said nothing, but the answer was written all over her unhappy little face. She wasn't grateful at all!

4

The "K" Word

J'll be honest. My feelings were hurt. But did I scold Snow White? No. Did I punish her? No! I simply instructed her to finish scrubbing the floor—at her own pace, I might add—before she took the rest of the day off. After that, I told myself, she could talk to the birds until she grew a beak, for all I cared.

Meanwhile, I retired to the palace. I checked my Magic Mirror, and its message was loud and clear: I looked frightful! It even told me Snow White was looking more attractive than I was! The awful stress of dealing with my ungrateful stepdaughter was taking its toll. I decided to take matters into my own hands.

So I decided to have a spa day. I canceled all my appointments and arranged for a massage and a seaweed wrap. Then, helped by meditation and aromatherapy, I fell into a deep, much-needed sleep.

The next morning, I awoke, completely refreshed. I was just about to consult my Magic Mirror to make sure that I was once again the fairest one of all when I heard a noise in the courtyard.

When I looked out my window, I saw Snow White at the well with her little bird friends. However, she wasn't drawing water. She was smiling and blushing at a young man who was standing a little too close to her!

The sight filled me with alarm. You know how boy crazy young girls can be. I crept closer to the window to get a better look.

What I saw was quite shocking. The young man seemed to have quite a keen interest in Snow White. He couldn't take his eyes off her. But why?

Then I had a chilling thought. What if the stranger had criminal intentions? What if he meant to do Snow White harm?

He could be a kidnapper!

Looking down at him, I thought of all the girls who had dropped out of sight recently—Little Red Riding Hood, Belle, that cute little Thumbelina—and I shuddered, fearing the worst.

Snow White might be lazy, and she definitely needed a better attitude, but I couldn't bear to think she might be in danger. I had to protect her!

5

Fresh Air

J fairly flew down the stairs, but by the time I reached Snow White, the stranger was gone. I was so relieved!

My stepdaughter felt differently. She had a bad case of the boy crazies and moped around for days, shirking her chores. I didn't know what to do. I started worrying again, and things took a turn for the worse. The Magic Mirror told me so in no uncertain terms.

"Snow White is the fairest one of all," it said.

"But what about me?" I asked.

"You need a makeover," it replied. I nearly wept.

Right around then, I began to think that perhaps a change of scenery might suit my dear little stepdaughter. She needed to get over her lovesickness and hop back on the healthy bandwagon.

Did that nice old woman in the gingerbread house have any room? I wondered. She lived on the other side of the forest, at least two days' walk from the palace.

And that's when I thought of Brad. I called him Brad the Huntsman because he was always roaming through the forest, hunting for mushrooms. He was a sweet man. Even though he wasn't the sharpest knife in the scullery, he knew the woods like the back of his hand.

Brad was just the person I needed! He could take Snow White deep into the forest, on a brisk nature walk. He could hunt for mushrooms, and she could pick wildflowers. Perfect! A long hike in the fresh air was bound to clear her head, I thought, and it would get her out of the palace for a few hours, which was a real plus.

I sent them off quickly. I don't mean to sound harsh, but I needed a break.

Instead, I got a massive shock. Because when Brad came back from the forest two hours later, he was alone.

Snow White had run away!

6
Runaway Girl

"What do you mean, she *ran away*?" I demanded, as Brad stood before me with his head bowed in shame. "You were supposed to take care of her! She's in danger out there! How could you let her wander off? And don't tell me again how many great mushrooms you found, Brad, because I just don't care!"

At this, the poor man burst into tears, and I realized it was pointless to scold him. Brad had done his best (and to give him credit, he *had* found some excellent, organic wild mushrooms), but Snow White had outwitted him. She'd run away—who knows why?—and now she was alone and defenseless in a place teeming with wild animals and—possibly—kidnappers.

There was only one way to rescue her.

I would have to do it myself.

I've heard so many ridiculous lies about the day I call "Operation Save Snow White" that I hardly know which one to tackle first. Perhaps I should start with the silliest of all—that I used black magic to disguise myself, so Snow White wouldn't recognize me. Nonsense!

It's true that I didn't wear my crown, or my robes, or my jewels that day, but why would I? To impress the chipmunks? No, I wore loose-fitting clothes and sturdy, comfortable shoes, suitable for the outdoors. And if I didn't do my hair or put on makeup—well, *excuse me*! I was going on a rescue mission, not a court visit!

So I set off into the forest. I would get a good hike in and do a good deed. What a great day I had in store!

Another silly rumor about that day is that I used black magic to find Snow White. Ridiculous. I didn't need it. She's a teenager, remember? All I had to do was follow the trail of hair bows and bubble-gum wrappers, straight to the little cottage in the forest.

That story about how I created a "poison apple" in the castle? Vicious gossip. I met a peddler along the way, who sold me a basket of shiny apples. Maybe I should have made sure they were organic, and pesticide-free, but I didn't. Nobody's perfect *all* the time.

7
A Wholesome Diet, Part 2

Well, Snow White was actually glad to see me, which was a pleasant surprise. She invited me in right away, and soon we were chatting comfortably by the fire. She told me that she liked my simple, homespun clothes, and that I looked a lot less intimidating without makeup.

"Really?" I asked. I was so touched!

"Yes," she said. And then she offered me some gooseberry pie. I may have mentioned my concerns about Snow White's health earlier. The girl just didn't know how to eat, and this was a perfect example.

"Pie for lunch?" I cried in dismay. How lucky I had run into that peddler! "Nothing could be worse for you! Put down that pie! Have some nice fresh fruit instead! Eat this apple." I offered her the shiniest one in my basket, knowing it would supply many of the vitamins and minerals so essential for normal growth.

Yes, that's why I gave her the apple—out of concern for her health. People have said I was trying to hurt her, even kill her, but they're wrong! And when Snow White fell into a deathlike swoon, it's true that I ran away, but only to find her a good gastroenterologist.

I never expected the search to take so long! You'd be surprised how few good doctors live in the forest. And once you find them, they refuse to make house calls. It's shocking.

Well, after hours of fruitless searching, I returned to the cottage, only to find it empty.

She's gone, I thought. There's nothing else I can do. So I began my mournful journey back to the palace, thinking that I might never see Snow White again, and that I would definitely sue the peddler who sold me those apples.

Then, to my amazement, I was suddenly being chased by seven of the nastiest little men you've ever seen. Shouting insults, claiming I had tried to harm their precious Snow White, they actually chased me to a rocky cliff. Me—the Queen!

Lightning crashed. I fell thousands of feet. Luckily, I landed on a soft patch of moss and only suffered a bruise or two—nothing very serious.

As I told you, I'm *very* healthy.

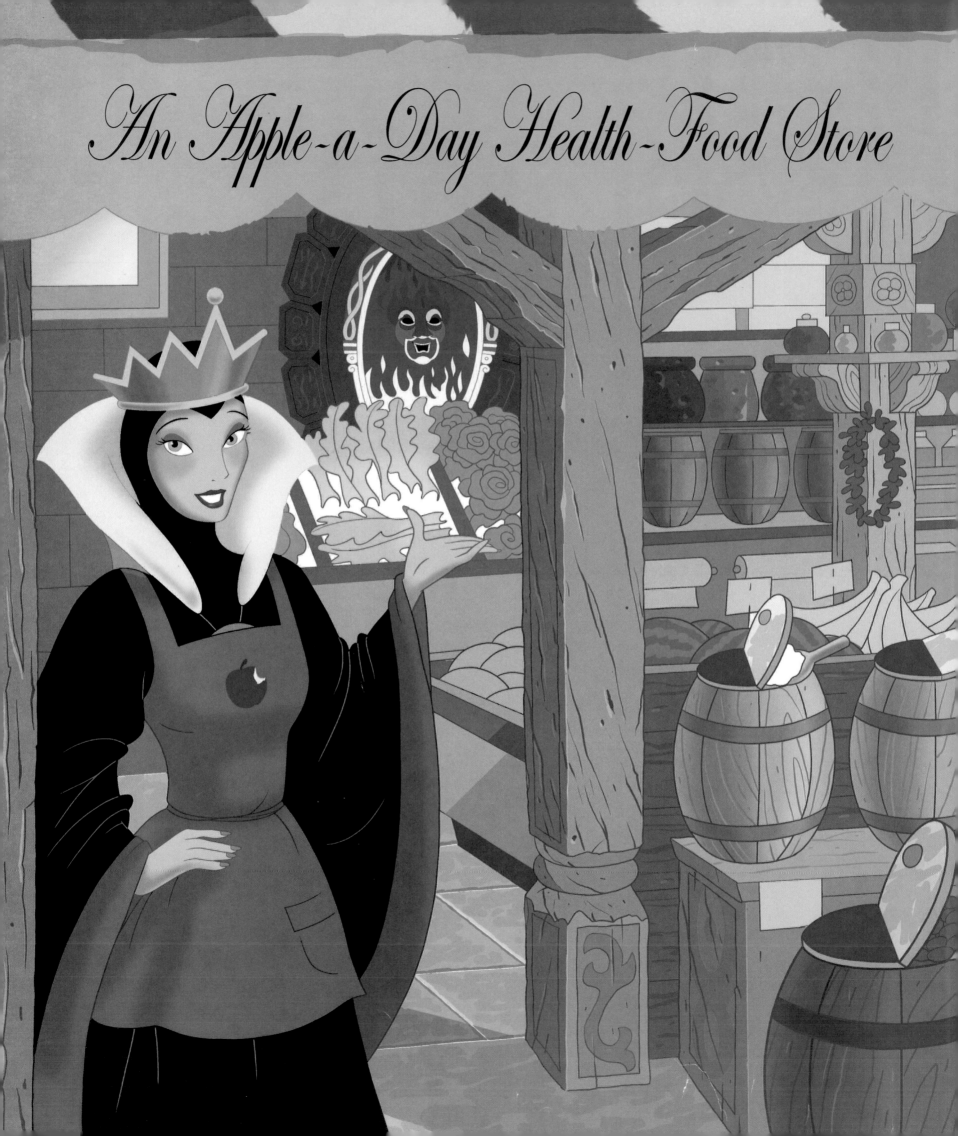

Now that you've heard my side of the story, I hope you'll think more kindly of me. Living in exile (the Dwarfs instigated a coup, and I was deposed) isn't so bad. I miss the power of the throne, but I don't miss all the stress and pressure that go with any busy ruler's job. I'm a lot calmer these days. I enjoy working in the health-food store, and I love giving the customers personal attention, especially when they need advice about what to eat.

Maybe you'll drop in some time?

MY SIDE of the Story

Printed in the United States of America

First Edition

10 9 8 7 6 5 4 3 2 1

Library of Congress Catalog Card Number: 2003103172

ISBN: 0-7868-3464-1

Visit www.disneybooks.com

MY SIDE of the Story

By *Snow White*

As told to Daphne Skinner

Illustrated by Atelier Philippe Harchy

Disney
PRESS

New York

1

Why I Don't Look Like a Princess

The main reason I don't look like a princess is that I spend all my time scrubbing and sweeping the palace. I don't mind cleaning. As a matter of fact, I like it. A lot. But the work is hard on my clothes. They're completely ragged. I haven't had a new dress since Father died, years and years ago.

Every time I ask the Queen, she says, "Don't be stupid, Snow White—you're still a growing girl!" The Queen is my stepmother, and my only parent now that Father is gone. She's very beautiful, but she has her moods, and I sometimes can't help feeling she doesn't like me very much.

Whenever she sees me, she scowls and gives me more work to do. Last week, she made me scrub the dungeon stairway three times. She told me it was good exercise.

And yesterday, when she saw me eating a bit of cake, she snatched it away.

"Sweets," she snapped, "are unsuitable for a growing girl. Stick to your diet of bread crusts and gruel, do you hear?"

I did.

This morning, as I drew water from the well, I found myself wondering if things would ever improve.

"Will the Queen like me better someday?" I asked my friends, the palace doves. "Will she give me a little time to myself, and something nice to eat?" They cocked their heads sweetly, as if considering the question.

"And will she let me have a new dress?" I said with a sigh. "I do hope so!"

2

My Dearest Wish

*T*he doves cooed, fluttering around the bucket as I hauled it up. I looked at them, wondering what they were trying to tell me. Then I understood. Why not make a wish? I was at a wishing well, after all!

So I stood there with my eyes closed and my fingers crossed, and I wished for the love of a kind, handsome prince, because that's what I *really* wanted, even more than tasty food and a new dress (though I wished for them, too, just in case).

Then, when I opened my eyes, the most wonderful thing happened. The handsomest young man I had ever seen was standing beside me at the well! He wore garments of silk and boots of softest leather. His hands and face were extremely clean. His shining brown locks were freshly washed and groomed. He looked like—a prince! A very clean one!

My heart raced. "Oh!" I exclaimed. Could it be that my dearest, most secret wish had truly been granted?

"Hello," he said. "Did I frighten you?"

I wanted to say no, but suddenly I was overwhelmed with shyness and couldn't speak a word.

Instead, I ran into the palace.

"Don't go!" he cried out with such longing that I hurried onto a balcony to wave to him. When one of the doves fluttered to my shoulder, I did something very bold. I kissed the dove and sent it down to the Prince!

At this he called, "I will never forget you!"

Then I saw the Queen.

She stood at her tower window, watching us. And something—perhaps the way her face was twisted into a grotesque snarl—told me she was not pleased. Not pleased at all.

3

The Huntsman Who Told a Lie

*B*eautiful as she was, the Queen could also be a teensy bit moody. Had I angered her? Would she punish me with some horrible new task, like sweeping out the dungeon, or polishing those terribly ugly gargoyles?

No, she would not.

Instead, the Queen sent word that I was to spend the day picking wildflowers with Brad the Huntsman! I was so relieved! She even gave me a new dress—and matching cape—to wear. It was almost too good to be true!

Putting down my scrub brush, I followed Brad into the forest, and before long I was happily gathering violets and field daisies.

"Aren't these beautiful?" I said, hearing Brad approach. "They're for the Queen. Have *you* found any pretty flowers, Brad?"

Brad said nothing. I looked up and found him standing over me, with a dagger in his hand.

"Brad!" I exclaimed. "You don't need a dagger to pick wild-flowers!"

He fell to his knees. "I can't do it," he said, with tears in his eyes. "I just can't!"

"That's all right," I said. "Don't cry! I'll give you some of mine."

"Forget the flowers!" he said. "The Queen commanded me to kill you, and I . . . I can't!"

"But—she would never do such a thing!" I protested. "Stop fibbing, Brad, or I might have to . . . scold you!"

"I'm not fibbing, Princess!" he insisted. "The Queen envies your beauty. She wants you dead! You must run away! Run and hide!" he implored between sobs.

I couldn't bear to see Brad in tears, so I gave in.

"All right," I said. "I'll find a place to hide, I promise. But please, stop crying!"

"Thank you, Princess," said Brad, brightening a little. Then, sniffling and wiping his eyes, he headed back to the palace.

4

Fright

As night fell, I began to wonder if I had made the right decision. The dark forest came alive in a most unsettling way. The wind moaned. Leaves rustled. I heard thuds, hoots, howls, squeaks, and cries.

I'm surrounded, I thought, shivering. But by what? I tried to make my way through the trees, tripping and stumbling. Branches grazed my arms. Thorns scratched my feet. Then something caught at my dress. Was it a hand? A claw? I pulled away in terror and heard a dreadful ripping sound.

"Oh, no!" I cried. "Not my *dress*! It's brand-new and it's the only one I have!"

Sobbing, I fell down in a swoon.

The handsome Prince with the shining hair leaned over me. "I love you, Snow White," he whispered, and his lips brushed my hand.

"I love you, too," I replied. He kissed my hand again, but now for some reason his nose was wet.

Then I woke up.

A little gray rabbit was nuzzling my hand. A fawn was leaning over me, ears pricked up. Birds watched from the trees, their eyes bright with concern. A squirrel tapped at my head with an acorn.

"Oh, my goodness!" I cried, remembering where I was, and all that had happened. "I'm all alone! I have no home! The Queen wants to kill me! And my dress is in shreds! What am I going to do?"

Three little bluebirds perched on a branch began to sing. A chipmunk pranced up to me and squeaked. A rabbit wiggled its nose. The fawn flicked its tail playfully.

"You're telling me not to worry, aren't you?" I asked. They nodded. Suddenly, I was ashamed of myself for being so fearful. Everything was going to be all right, especially if I could find a place to stay.

"Do you know of any cottages for rent?" I asked.

They shook their little heads.

"Oh," I said, trying not to sound too disappointed. "Well, I'm sure I'll find something."

But where? I wondered.

Then, as if answering my question, the bluebirds flew down, took hold of my tattered skirt, and began leading me through the forest.

5

Dirt

"Oh, how adorable!" I cried. Nestled in the trees ahead of us, just beyond a rushing brook, was the dearest little cottage I had ever seen.

I couldn't wait to find out who lived there, so I hurried across the bridge, and knocked at the door.

"Hello!" I called. "May I come in?" Hearing no answer, I peered through the windows, which were so dusty that I had to rub at them with my already tattered skirt.

It was dark inside.

I tried the door. It was unlocked! I tiptoed in, followed by a crowd of animals and birds. At first, all I could see were some tiny chairs—seven of them.

Could seven children be living here? I wondered. How strange! I looked around a little more, and saw a sink and a fireplace with a kettle hanging in it. Then, as my eyes became accustomed to the gloom, I received a hideous shock.

The sink was full of dirty dishes, cobwebs hung from every corner, and the floor was covered with dust. The place was filthy!

"We've got to clean this cottage," I announced to my companions. "How can those poor children live like this?"

So we all got busy, scrubbing and sweeping and polishing. The birds and animals were so helpful—dusting furniture with their tails, pulling down cobwebs with their beaks, washing dishes with their little paws—that everything was sparkling in no time.

"I wish you'd been with me at the palace," I told them when the last dish was put away. "You are *such* good workers!" I looked around with satisfaction. What had once been a horrible mess was now wonderfully clean and tidy.

"Let's take a short break," I continued, "and then we'll head upstairs."

I'm ashamed to say that when we did go upstairs, the sight of seven dear little beds lined up in a row made me forget all my good intentions. Cleaning would have to wait, I decided. It was time for a rest.

Yawning, I read the names that were carved into the footboards: Doc, Sleepy, Sneezy, Happy, Dopey, Bashful, and Grumpy.

"What odd names for children!" I mused.

There were squeaks and twitters of agreement. Then all of us—chipmunks, squirrels, fawns, raccoons, rabbits, and bluebirds—settled down for a nice long nap.

6

A Fine How-Do-You-Do

The handsome Prince took my hand and kissed it. His fingernails were so clean! "I love you, Snow White," he whispered.

"I love you, too," I said.

He smiled, revealing gleaming white teeth. Then he said something, but a noise, almost like very loud whispering, drowned out his voice.

"What did you say?" I asked.

His lips moved again. I couldn't hear a word.

"PLEASE, SPEAK UP!" I shouted. "I CAN'T HEAR YOU!"

And then I awoke.

The seven little children were peering at me over the foot of the beds. They were very strange children indeed. They had beards and they were filthy! I couldn't help it. I screamed!

I fought the urge to jump out of bed and scrub each and every one of them with a stiff brush. Instead, I managed to say, "How do you do?"

"How do you do *what*?" snapped one of them. I took a closer look. He wasn't a dirty, bearded child. He was a dwarf! There were seven of them!

He's awfully grumpy, I thought. And then I realized: he *was* Grumpy!

It didn't take long to match the others to their names. The one with the big grin was Happy. The one who kept yawning was Sleepy. The one with the spectacles was Doc. The one who sneezed so hard that the curtains flapped was Sneezy. The one who blushed when I looked at him was Bashful, and the one with big blue eyes was Dopey. He looked, well, kind of . . . dopey.

Grumpy glared at me. "We know who *we* are," he said. "Who are *you*, and what are you doing here?"

I introduced myself, and then I told them about picking wildflowers with Brad the Huntsman. "He said my stepmother the Queen wants to kill me, but I just can't believe it. I don't like to say this," I said, leaning forward, "but I think Brad was fibbing."

"Maybe not," said Doc. "The Queen is lawful. I mean awful."

"She's bad," said Happy.

"She's an old witch full of black magic," said Grumpy to the six other little men. "And if she finds *her* here," he added, pointing at me, "we're done for!"

"But she'll never find me here," I protested. "And if you let me stay, I'll keep your house very, very clean."

They backed away as one. I could see this was the wrong argument, so I tried again.

"I—I'll cook for you. I'll give you good healthy food, like bread and gruel!"

"Bread and gruel?" echoed Happy. He beckoned to the others and they went into a huddle. After a long, whispered discussion, Doc stepped forward.

"What about apple dumplings?" he asked. "Will you make those?"

"As many as you like," I promised.

They cheered—even Grumpy—and we all hurried downstairs.

"There's only one condition," I told them when we reached the kitchen. "Before you sit down at the table, you have to wash."

"Wash?" Sleepy's eyes flew open. Happy's smile disappeared. The other dwarfs looked dismayed, too.

"We did wash," they said.

"When?"

"Last week."

"Last month."

"Last year."

"Recently."

I saw that I was going to have to be very firm with them. "March straight outside and wash, or you won't get anything to eat, not even bread and gruel."

They marched.

7

The Strange Old Lady and Her Very Shiny Apple

Our meal of apple dumplings, plum pudding, and gooseberry pies would have horrified the Queen, for it wasn't the least bit wholesome. But it was a lot tastier than bread and gruel, and it gave us all a chance to get acquainted.

The Dwarfs told me about their work down in the diamond mines. I told them about life at the palace, and my wish at the well.

"And it did come true," I said. "It brought me a handsome prince—for a few minutes, anyway." I sighed, suddenly overcome with yearning. How I hoped I would I see the Prince again—for more than a few minutes.

Then the clock began to strike. "It's bedtime!" I cried. "Go right upstairs, all of you!"

"You can have our beds," offered Doc.

"We'll sleep down here," said Sleepy.

"Oh, I couldn't do that!" I said, but they insisted. Once I saw that the dear little men were perfectly comfortable sleeping in the sink, in cupboards, on the floor, and in cooking vats, I gave in.

I climbed the stairs, and before I fell asleep, I said a silent thanks for my seven adorable new friends. Then I slept.

The next morning, as the Dwarfs got ready for work, they warned me to be careful while they were down in the mines.

"The Queen's a sly one," said Doc, "so beware of strangers."

"Oh, don't worry about me," I said, touched by their concern. "I'll be just fine." Nothing could possibly go wrong on such a beautiful day, I thought, as I kissed them each good-bye on the forehead. It was sunny and bright, perfect for airing out the cottage and doing some serious housework. I could hardly wait to pick up a broom!

With the help of the birds and the animals, who came rushing into the cottage as soon as the Dwarfs were gone, I scrubbed and swept and dusted, and then I scrubbed some more.

"I can hardly believe we cleaned this place yesterday," I said to the birds. "Can you?"

They couldn't, either.

At last, everything was sparkling and tidy, and it was time to start baking. Tonight, I had decided, we would have fruit pies for dessert. I began to roll out the crust.

"Peach or cherry?" I mused. "Rhubarb or apple?"

Before I could make up my mind, a strange old woman appeared at the door.

"Making pies?" she asked. She had a huge wart on her nose, which was not the slightest bit attractive. I tried very hard not to stare at it.

"Yes, I am," I said, making my decision. "*Gooseberry* pies."

"Why not use some of these?" she asked, showing me the apples in her basket. "They're delicious! Taste one. Go on, have a bite."

The apple she offered looked lovely (and it was extremely clean), but as I reached for it, the oddest thing happened. The birds—the same sweet little birds who had been helping me with the housework—flew at the old woman, as if they were attacking her!

She dropped the apple with a croak, and before I could stop her, she was down on her hands and knees, searching for it. At last, after many earsplitting cries of woe, she found it. She wiped it clean as carefully as if it were a precious jewel.

I felt very sorry for the poor old thing—the threat of losing one of her apples had shaken her so! I helped her up, and because she was none too steady on her feet, I invited her into the cottage.

Her spirits improved quickly once we were inside, and again she offered me the apple.

"I'll tell you a secret," she said, holding it just beyond my reach. "This is no ordinary apple. It's a magic wishing apple. One bite and all your dreams will come true."

"A magic wishing apple? Does it work like a wishing well?" I asked hopefully.

"Much better!" she assured me. "There's no comparison! Now go on," she urged, placing the apple in my hand. "Make your wish and take a nice big bite."

And so I did.

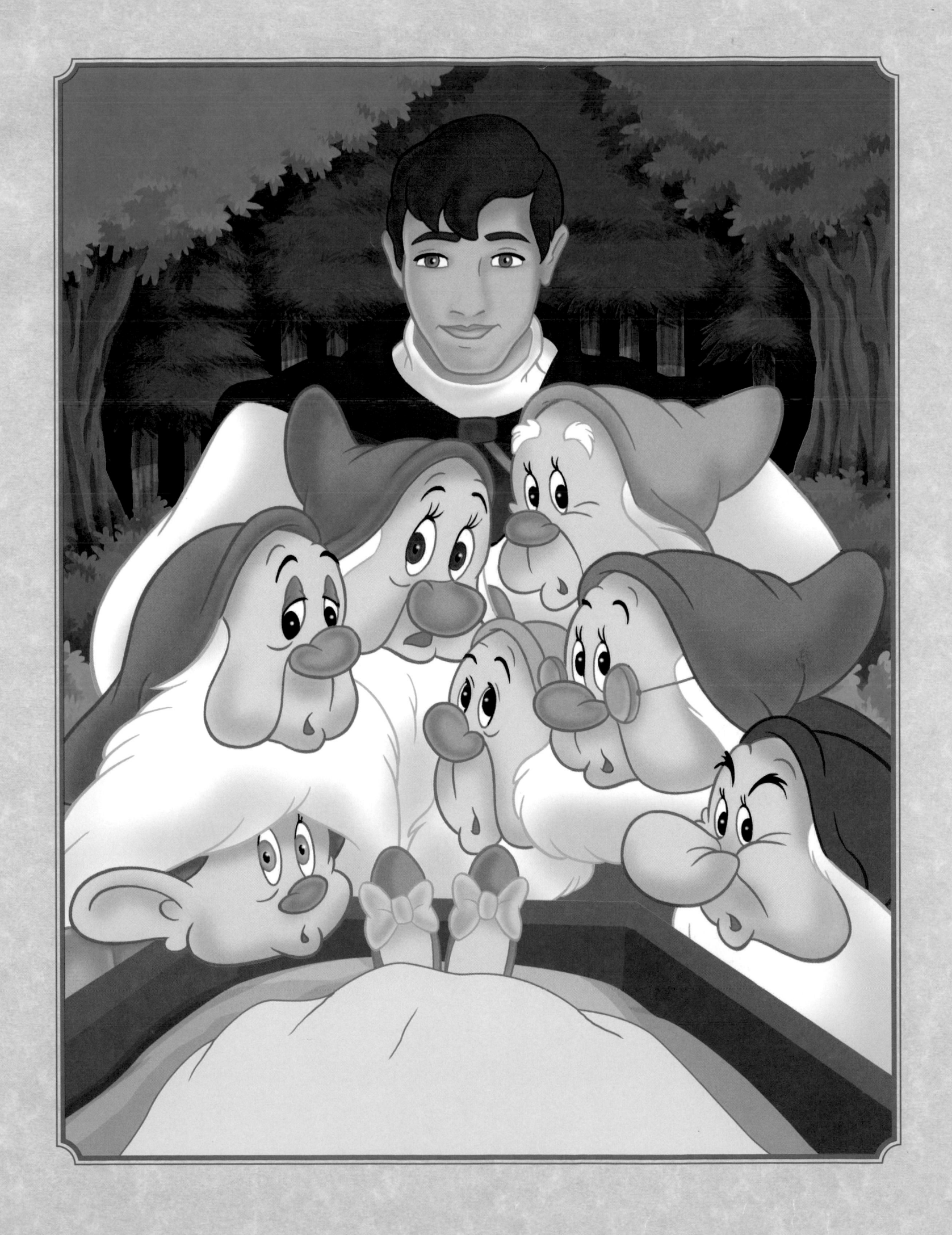

My Dearest Wish, Part 2

The handsome Prince leaned over and kissed me. His lips were as soft as a dove's wing. I opened my eyes, and there he was, kneeling at my side!

I must be dreaming, I thought. And then I wondered—what am I doing in a glass coffin? But I didn't have time to find out because the next thing I knew, the Prince took my hand, and his touch made my heart thump like a clean sheet flapping in the wind.

I stood. We embraced. He told me that he loved me. I told him that I loved him. The birds sang. The Dwarfs cheered, wiping tears from their grimy little faces as I bade them farewell.

Then I rode away with my handsome prince, waving good-bye to the sweet little Dwarfs and those nice clean animals.

We got married, and those Dwarfs gave us the nicest wedding gift ever (they do work in a diamond mine, you know). And I got to wear a brand-new dress—a big white one. That was the best part of all.

The Prince and I lived happily ever after—and it's all thanks to the old woman with the huge yucky wart and the apple. I never saw her again, but I'd love to thank her. That wishing apple really *did* work!